MW00982344

A Time to Cry

POEMS BY

Paul Kloschinsky

TRAFFORD
PUBLISHING

USA ▪ Canada ▪ UK ▪ Ireland

Note for Librarians: A cataloguing record for this book is available from Library and Archives
Canada at www.collectionscanada.ca/amicus/index-e.html
ISBN 1-4120-9928-5

Printed in Victoria, BC, Canada. Printed on paper with minimum 30% recycled fibre.
Trafford's print shop runs on "green energy" from solar, wind and other environmentally-friendly power sources.

TRAFFORD
PUBLISHING™
Offices in Canada, USA, Ireland and UK

Book sales for North America and international:
Trafford Publishing, 6E–2333 Government St.,
Victoria, BC V8T 4P4 CANADA
phone 250 383 6864 (toll-free 1 888 232 4444)
fax 250 383 6804; email to orders@trafford.com
Book sales in Europe:
Trafford Publishing (UK) Limited, 9 Park End Street, 2nd Floor
Oxford, UK OX1 1HH UNITED KINGDOM
phone +44 (0)1865 722 113 (local rate 0845 230 9601)
facsimile +44 (0)1865 722 868; info.uk@trafford.com
Order online at:
trafford.com/06-1685

10 9 8 7 6 5 4 3

To my parents, without whose love and support I would most surely have perished.

I
The Mad Medic

My Mind Howls

My mind howls at the night.
Ablaze with vibrant colors,
in conversation with ghosts,
attacked by bands of thieves,
a withdrawal into my labyrinth,
in heroic struggle with slippery beasts,
grasping women who vanish,
the urban lights a sensuous seduction.
Leading me to wander
through cold city streets,
where my hunger is unsatisfied,
and irritable from my failure
I become autistic and perplexed
and they drag me to the hospital
and put me on medicine.

The Broken Machine

My computer worked fine
for a long time.
It processed data,
crunched numbers
and performed sophisticated tasks;
breezing through the things
it was required
to do.

> (The class all took notes
> but he resisted,
> instead listening to
> professor;
> He was the first
> to finish the exam
> and received one of the
> best marks.)

My computer started to act up
one day; making funny sounds,
becoming slow and quirky,
like it contracted a virus,
until it crashed completely
leaving me helpless.

(The lunatic wandered the streets
forgetting his daily tasks
and worrying his family.)

I took the machine to the repair shop
and they installed special software
to get it up and running again.

(He didn't know what hit him
but he took the medicine).

I worked a while on the repaired machine
until one day it crashed again.
I wished I could get another
computer that was more reliable,
but it was the only one I could afford,
it having been given to me
by an old, bearded man
who worked for
a manufacturer.

("Not this again"
he exclaimed
as they showed him
his hospital room.)

I feared the old man
had it in for me
having given me a model
that doesn't work well
according to the people
at the repair shop.

(He sat on his hospital bed
wondering if he would
ever live again.)

I found out from the shop
that my computer could crash again
at any time.

(The lunatic watched
the ball bounce
back and forth
between the children
playing outside
his window.)

So how can I rely
on a machine that could
malfunction at any time?

Perhaps it could crash now,
perhaps it could crash later,
perhaps it could crash
never again.

(At home the lunatic
took his pills,
frightened
for his future.)

It is frightening,
the uncertainty of not
knowing if the damn thing
will crash again.
I rely on it for my life
and work,
like a carpenter
on his saw, hammer
and nails.

(Feeling better
he took a job.
But still the doubts lingered.)

So how do I go on?

The knowledge that
my life could fall apart
at any time
if I'm too dependent
on the special software
to keep the damn thing running
and realize my dreams;
when I could suddenly be cast
into the hell
of utter frustration.

Medication Time

I take the pills daily.
Tiny tablets to keep me sane,
slay dragons,
ward off evil spirits,
defend against wild
Dionysian dismemberment,
chemical Lancelots
to protect my mind.
But then there's the things
they cannot do—
rebuild shattered social networks,
give back lost dysfunctional years,
let me be who I want to be.
But they do offer a release,
taken in excess they provide
an eternal slumber.
The tiny tablets giving
an escape from life,
an option I'd rather not take
but might have to explore
if reality bites too hard.

A Traditional Club

The nakedness of woman is the work of God.
William Blake

It's a cheap place.
Assaulting your senses—
the taste of cold beer
and cigarettes.
The sound of overpowering
modern music
and cheering men.
The sight of neon lights,
sports TV,
cherry blossoms,
a flashing stage with a hot tub,
and women,
dancing,

naked.

A tarnished glimpse of heaven
and evolutionary power.
A testament to Man's eternal fascination
with the female form,
and God's enduring genius.

I know some would
worship him in a church
but I would prefer to worship him
in a glorious sunrise
or in a dimly lit, smoky bar
at the altar of
women.

A Lunatic's Abyss

I could have been a contender.
I had the good life
medical degree,
girlfriends,
confidence,
but then like a train wreck
life blind sided me.
Striping me of my independence,
my sanity,
my social identity,
my belief in myself,
and my God.
And now She sits silent
acting all high and mighty
like a disinterested lover
oblivious to my cries.

Some say it's through suffering
that we learn and become wise,
like spiritual basic training,
but all it feels like
is a slide backwards

into a bottomless pit.

And try as I might to climb out

the walls just crumble in my fingers

and I slide deeper still

into the abyss.

A Gentle Dionysos

I was thrown into the caldron of desire
where I drank a wild, ecstatic, excessive brew.
With feelings that raged like a bonfire,
intuitions that howled like the wind,
sensations that felt like the quaking earth,
and thoughts that flowed like
the tributaries of a flooding river.
Until I stumbled back into the world
gently embracing the ones I hold dear.
Searching for my love Ariadne,
to channel my passions to their goal
and soothe my dismembered mind
with a bond to last the ages.

Solitude

Forgive me if I don't fit in
with those who converse easily.
Its not I'm a snob
or dismissive of companionship,
just soft spoken and silent
preferring to think before I speak.

Keeping things to myself,
sometimes unsure of my opinion
needing time for them to blossom,
nurtured in the soil of solitude.

Where the lone wolf howls
and they can grow wild,
free from any pruning
from harsh critical eyes,
my soul thus refreshed
by a well formed bud of a thought.

So don't judge me too quickly
and forgive me these sins
of an introvert.

Companionship Shock

I was so pleased to get your call,
piercing the darkness of my state,
releasing me from a straightjacket
of binding turmoil.
Through all my mad incarnations
and raging at the world
you stuck by me like the moon
circles the earth faithfully,
caring about my life,
encouraging me to go on,
blessing me with a friendship
that in my time of dire need
was worth more to me than the stars.

A Lowly Fancy

I'm sitting drinking a beer
in some neighborhood pub,
feeling rather strange
as the patrons watch the World Cup
and I sit thinking about Dante
when I notice the waitress,
working hard,
probably receiving scant reward
for all her efforts.

And I wonder about her flights of fancy
or the dreams of anyone in here.
Will they take flight and survive,
soaring high with wild indulgence,
or will they be flushed away
like this beer will be
after it passes through my body
and hits the urinal basin

Crash Landing

It was a lively flight.
Engaging conversation,
laughs aplenty,
good cheer,
but at the request of my doctor
the pilot throttled down
and refueled with anti psychotics
until the plane descended abruptly
and crash landed.

And now I sit charred in the wreckage,
my friends but a memory,
with the sirens and flashing lights
of reality hosing me down.

And as I strain for a glimpse
of a rewarding tomorrow
my heart hangs heavy
as a lead ornament,
and my dreams stick like soot
to my boots.

Rented Body

The siren call of the city's bright lights
Seduces me to abandon my safe home.
Enslaved to the visions that walk in the night
Restless and sad from too much time alone.
Though some say its not right to heed the call
The painted faces and adorned bodies burn in my mind,
'Till I search for a woman who has taken the fall
Not caring about my station or what is my kind.
I know you can't offer me much more than a thrill
A Mephistophilian journey on dark city streets
The neon lights blazing like I'm on some exotic pill
My money the only introduction for us to meet.
Its been so very long since I've been laid
The only women I can get want to be paid.

Doubt

I used to believe,
a child listening to a childlike religion,
the sermons,
Sunday school lessons,
and resurrection stories
comforting me while I slept.

Then I studied a profession
and my faith was buried
under a pile of anatomy charts
and patho-physiological mechanisms.
Until one day my neurochemistry attacked me,
stripping me of my mental health
and my hope dwindled to a mere pilot light
kept lit by my fledgling faith.

And even this threatens
to crumble like a sandcastle
bombarded by the tidal waters
of circumstance.

So I pray for a God with enough potency
to resurrect my decrepit life
and once and for all put to rest
these spasms of doubt.

Deception

I found out my companion was false.
Where once he showered me with praise
confirming my deepest desires,
now his words were revealed to be a pack of lies,
like the fog lifting to reveal a charging bull.

Confirming my deepest fears,
leaving me to use my wit and reason,
to sift through the deceptive waste
and pierce the side of the raging beast.

Social Isolation

I stumbled alone in the forest,
madness my only companion.

My former friends abandoning me,
their affection fading

like rats from a sinking ship.
Now that I've found my way

they remain nowhere to be found.
So I must start from scratch,

spinning a social network
like a spider spinning a web.

But its hard to make anything stick.
So am I to become a recluse?

Or should I spin patiently,
a strand here and there,

hoping my craft steers true
and I can enjoy companionship once again.

Support Group

They gather like hobos
warming themselves
around a fire at night.
Each one gathering some wood
to throw on the fire
to warm the others.
Bonded together by their
common experience and pain,
huddling close to share stories.

But I have a hard time finding twigs
to contribute to the flames
being soft spoken by disposition
and not being able to express
my somewhat unique experiences easily.

So I drift away from the group,
and say a prayer,
for a companion I can trust,
and try to make a small solitary fire
to warm myself until sunrise.

The Set Trap's Teeth

They dragged me from my bed,
the police spraying pepper spray,
my eyes burning like red hot gritty sand.
With voices assaulting me on the inside
and the cops barking orders on the outside.
I stumbled blinded around my room,
until they handcuffed me
and led me to the ambulance.
My tranquillity destroyed
like a fish on a hook.

I thought they were taking me to the forest
where they would then dismember me,
but instead they drove me to the hospital.
There they stripped off my clothes
and strapped me to a bed.
I thought I was in hell
and the nurse was a demon
poking me with a hypodermic pitchfork.
And the devil was going to sodomize me.

So I screamed,
and fought,
convinced I was in a titanic struggle

with pure evil.
Until the medicine kicked in
and I drifted off to sleep.

I later awoke,
realized my horror was
pure fantasy
and shook it all off
like a bad dream.

Lost

They drag them in
from all over the city.
Like solders gone AWOL,
not from the military,
but rather from society.
Unable to function,
precipitating out.
and landing in the
emergency room.

Once in the hospital
they take their medicine,
pace the halls,
and rummage through ashtrays.
Taking the scant tobacco
from used cigarette butts
to roll a smoke.

And they pray for
a restoration of their dignity.
Like a recovering alcoholic,
or a not guilty verdict.

But so many are lost,
penniless and alone,
and remain forsaken,
by even God himself.

Shrink

As cool as a steel blade
they cut up your life.
Carving it up
into easily digested bits.
Engaging in name calling—
manic, psychotic, depressed, schizoid.
Until your individuality is buried,
like a fingerprint worn down,
by therapeutic and prognostic implications.
Rummaging through your past
for any sign of spirit.
Demanding explanations
for eccentric deeds
or just plain fun.
Wary of anyone
who lives more than they do.
Them in their risk free
sanitized lives.
Leaving you with a label;
a leaky boat plugged,
but moored to the shore.

Hospital

The brightest part of the day
was getting my dinner tray
of hospital food
which was bland as the desert.
But like Pavlov's dog
I learned to salivate anyways
at the sound of the dinner bell.
Which rescued me
from pacing the halls,
like a hamster on it's wheel,
while the red exit sign
blazed like some exotic neon light;
or sitting in the smoking lounge
my head full of voices,
like a noisy boardroom,
being cut off from the others.
And regularly the nurses
brought me my medicine
which I was blissfully unaware
held the key
to my subsequent parole.

Psychologist

We talked and talked and talked.
About my mood,
my voices,
my prospects.
And when we tired of that—
existential psychology,
choice,
responsibility.

Ventilating my mind
like a patient on
an empathetic respirator.

Until I grew weary,
my life unfolding
independently of our discussions.

So I took my leave,
as a voice whispered to me
"God is the psychoanalyst for the hero."

Voice

I have a voice in my head
who says I'm fine.
But I don't believe him.

He tells me wonderful things—
I'm smart,
creative,
talented,
good looking.
But I don't believe him.

I once had a bad voice
who cut me to pieces.
I sometimes believed him.

So on we go like Siamese twins.
Sharing the same brain,
feelings,
perceptions,
and memories.
And he says I'm OK.
But I don't believe him.

I'm waiting for a real person,

one I can trust,

to say some of the same things.

Then I might believe them.

Stigma

Don't forget me
or discriminate against me;
simply because I have an illness
that flares like a sunspot
while the star shines on bright.
Rendering me temporarily disabled,
like a person with a fractured limb,
that heals strong with proper care.

Although I'm not normal in my episodes,
I certainly can make a claim
to normality when I'm well.

So welcome me like a prodigal son,
who has wandered through the desert,
battling demons,
slaying dragons,
on a hair raising adventure,
who now must return
to his friends and family
and their loving care;

before entering the world
as a lucid participant.

Riverview

I worked there as a doctor
at the notorious mental institution
where the patients gorged themselves
on tap water
enough to make them drunk.
I tried to help
but the patients were very sick
modern psychiatry having failed
to make them acceptable to society
like a student being failed
by multiple teachers
until they are permanently expelled
or like a sinking ship
descending to the bottom
where others might float.

They now lay rusting away
in a hellish environment.
So I didn't last long there
once my psychiatric
curiosity was satisfied
and left one day

only to find
that I would soon be
mentally ill myself
and hoping I would float.

Father

He loves me deeply.
I can tell it in his eyes.

Like when he hugs me
and gently prods me
to go to the hospital
when I'm engulfed in psychotic fire.
Or when he looked frantically for me
when I was late returning to the hospital.
Combing the city streets,
desperate as an addict looking for his drugs,
eventually finding me in a strip club.
Where he calmly bought me a beer
before leading me back.

I hope I haven't been
too much of a disappointment
these past, desperate years
and I can someday
make him proud again.
But I suspect he might be already.
I only hope I can one day
give my own family
a heart as big as his.

Faith

I thought I had it nailed.
From observing creation
and the improbable nature
of the circumstances
that have led to
life on this planet.
Then I observed the
improbabilities that have
occurred in my own life
and my own share of what
some would call luck.

So I believed.

Then fate blind-sided me
with a most unwelcome
development.
And I wept.
And lost my faith.

Until one day
it occurred to me
that a creator capable
of creating the bounty

of this earth, is capable
of ends and means
incomprehensible to me,
but perhaps for my benefit.

So I believed again.

And I vowed to submit myself
to the divine will.
And like poor Job of old
to have unshakable faith.

On My Own

Sorry, but that's where I want to be.
Away from the prying eyes,
removed from the needless chatter,
surrounded by my books,
my art,
my music;
getting closer to God,
lost in my thoughts,
responsible for no one but myself.

Sure, I still need companionship,
and need someone to share my
ups and downs with.

But most of the time
I'll prefer privacy
to a party
and leave the social graces for those
more inclined to such things.
I just hope I get over the guilt
of following a solitary path,
so I can enjoy my independence,
like a lone mountain peak,
and let a cherished few come close
who respect my right to be me.

Quarrel

It seems so trivial,
the reason we squared off.
Things were going well,
then we disagreed
and tempers flared
like the winds
in a tropical storm.
Leaving me to wonder
what went wrong
and why we lash out
at those we love the most.

As a failed project
or the bottom line
can tear us apart,
so I hope the years between us
will bind us together.
And we can forget
this incident,
replacing it with
happier memories
and know that family
comes before any feud.

My Parent's Grief

I was too busy chasing demons
to even notice them.

The shining lights of the city
reflected on the water
like a candlelight vigil.

Then the attacks by the rabid beasts;
with the fights,
and crucifixions,
and confusion.

It was only later
in the hospital,
bound and medicated,
that I noticed—

my father's graying hair,
my mother's wrinkling face,

and the deep sorrow
and concern

in both their eyes;

blanketing me like
Mary at Jesus's
death.

Scenes

Its been so long
since we were together.
Once we laughed,
and studied,
and drank;
our lives securely intertwined
by common experience and goals
like soldiers going into battle.

Then we did part
promising to keep in touch
but now I can't remember
the last time we talked.
Our lives are so different now
and like you the scenes
have come and gone
the passing years disintegrating
all but the most durable bonds.

Bars

I relive each day,
each month,
each year
of my illness,
like a prisoner
counting the days
until his release.
My prison being
not made of bars
but rather social isolation.

I don't know the length
of my sentence,
so I sit and ruminate
whether I am making
progress; and if the days
will bring, like that prisoner
facing parole, the promise
of a better tomorrow.
One filled with camaraderie
and the precious gift
of normality.

Sub-Par

I used to have peaks
and valleys in my life.
Then the valleys got deeper
and the peaks shorter.
Until it was all averaged out,
by medicine,
and I'm stuck with a
sub-par life in a rut.

With no change,
endlessly,
incessantly,
like the moon and stars,
or the mountains and sea.
Except my life lacks their beauty
and just shares their exasperating
stubbornness.
And as the days turn into months,
and the months to years,
and the years to decades,
it seems certain nothing will change,
and I will just live this constricted life,
like a cesspool,
watching the rivers flow.

Listening

I was always different from my peers.
We hung out together but
they frequently mocked my silent
and solitary ways.
And I loved but unfortunately was
not able to possess my beloved.
Then finally I became mad,
requiring heroics, hospitalizations
and medicine.

Now that the turmoil has settled
I find myself alone,
so dreadfully alone.
And my only hope is in a
benevolent deity that can
give me a satisfactory life.
If I'm being punished
I know not for what
and would gladly stand
in front of my accusers.

But in the end I just pray,
like a graduating student,

for companionship
and rewarding work.

And hope someone is listening.

II
The Black Labyrinth

Nowhere to Run

I go through the motions
getting up, going to work, doing my best;
trying to think good thoughts.
But still the sorrow endures—
my heart feeling heavy,
my body burning,
as if my blood were molten lava.
What good is life without fun?
Trapped with nowhere to run.

I take the medicine,
which takes away the violent dismemberment
and lets me make a stab at sanity.
But still the sorrow endures—
with clouded pessimistic thinking,
despair,
and self reproach.
What good is life without fun?
Trapped with nowhere to run.

I tell myself that it will pass
and pray for a steady hand
to direct my fate safely.
But still the sorrow endures—

feeling like it will never end,
mocking my best hopeful thoughts,
robbing me of my future.
What good is life without fun?
Trapped with nowhere to run.

Lonely

I live a solitary life
not by choice
but rather by condemnation;
my neurochemistry forcing me
to spend my time alone
and I'm lonely,
lonely as the moon.

My former lovers are as distant
as a far away galaxy;
the memory of their faces
assault me daily
and I ask myself,
will it ever end?
…even prisoners don't stay
in solitary confinement forever.

So I'll stuff my verse in a bottle
and throw it in the sea
surrounding my desert island.
And pray somebody reads it.
And pray somebody cares.

Blue

Today was just another day
no worse than all the rest.
Nothing happened that could be
construed as ill fortune
although nothing happened
that was welcome also.
Yet still my mood did sink
and I started to think foul thoughts.
I don't know why I feel so blue
but despite everything still I do.

I guess something positive could
lift my spirits upward.
But then again I have a lot
to be thankful for.
Usually a serenity of mind
and security are my welcome
companions, leading me to
count my blessings.
I don't know why I feel so blue
but despite everything still I do.

So how do I find relief?
In a pill, a bottle or positive

self talk? It seems irrational
that my spirits are so independent
of my situation. Yet still they
weigh me down when I'm on course
and enjoying calm seas. My dark
predictions may themselves cause ruin.
I don't know why I feel so blue
but despite everything still I do.

So forgive me if I don't cheer up
as quickly as I usually do.
But despite the outward
circumstances I sometimes see
the world through dark,
pessimistic glasses, even though
any rational evaluation would
lead me to be cheerful indeed.
I don't know why I feel so blue
but despite everything still I do.

Drizzle

It seems like it will never end.
The incessant pitter patter
on the the window pane.
The puddles forming a patchwork,
outside my window,
from the endless downpour.

And it leaves me wondering
about my state:
human, yes,
alive,
but what else?

The tedious onslaught
of mundane duties
and soggy schedules
makes me feel like
getting into bed
and pulling the covers
over my head.
Unless I find something lasting,
something meaningful,
to stop the drizzle.

Despair

It rises like floodwater
a stinking cesspool of negative attitudes,
cynicism and pessimism
clouding my vision,
drowning my future
in self-reproach and hopelessness.

So I pack sandbags
of accurate cognitive beliefs,
piling them high
to guard against the filthy water
and pray my hope survives.

Confidence

I hit the mark today
but not without some apprehension
my insecurities assaulting me
like the wind bending a tree sideways.

But the trunk did not break
and I was able to perform my task
and take one small baby step
towards reaching my goals.

Gallows

Why must I suffer continually
when I have been convicted of nothing?

Still I stand like a condemned man
at the gallows
noose around my neck,
trapdoor quivering under my weight.

Will the hangman pull the lever
or will God give me a last minute reprieve?
And let me live my life
with a heart that sings,
a mind like quicksilver,
and a spirit that soars
above these wasted, condemned years.

Marilyn

I have a picture of her above my bookshelf.
Sitting on a doorstep,
mini skirt, fishnet stockings,
the shoulder of her blouse
pulled down,
and a look in her eyes
that promises eternal bliss.
I remember hearing that
she had problems with low self esteem,
and I wonder if
worldwide adoration
does not bring self respect,
then what hope do I,
a person with a mental illness,
have of achieving self esteem.

Then I think of a few
of the people I know personally.
None with a particular claim to fame.
Some who are poised and confident.
And I feel more optimistic
that someday I too,
like them,
can experience
self love.

Patience

I must be patient
to weather the storms
that threaten my existence.
Patient as ivy.
Slowly growing towards
its chosen path
in the darkness
waiting for a companion sprout
going in the same direction,
maybe a friend
not knowing if they will ever come.

So on I go toiling in the shadows
far from the flickering lights
of the skyline or sun.
Not knowing when I'll find companionship
just persistently growing
day after day
on this lonely path.

A Time to Cry

I shed a tear today,
as the storm clouds gathered
and the wind blew the leaves
from the naked, mist shrouded trees.

I ruminated about my lost life—
my self,
my loves,
my future,
my sins.

And as I ruminated with these thoughts,
I excavated some emotions,
and unearthed some buried
ideas and dreams,
that I took some tentative steps
to show to the light of day.

When I did
my spirit soared,
and I realized that
like punishing a child,
melancholy can have
a beneficial
effect.

Hopeless

I'm stranded on a desert island.
And as the days, months, years grind on
my hope of rescue vanishes,
dwindling until it is as faint
and distant as the North Star.
While the demons in my head
betray me once again.

And like a man chasing a mirage
through the desert
my thirst is unsatisfied,
and my drive is frustrated.
Desperation becomes my only companion
and just when I think I can't go on any farther
I'm forced to endure even more.

So I pray to the heavens,
but fear no one is listening,
and I will waste away
vanishing without a trace.

Courage

I'm so afraid
of what I don't know—
maybe my future,
maybe my past,
maybe the inevitable uncertainty
that any mentally ill person
must always face.

So like a deer in the headlights
I remain frozen.
Paralyzed by depressive inertia,
I hope for the courage
to overcome this fear
and despair
and act decisively,
darting out of the way,
avoiding disaster,
fleeing to safety.
And be able to live carefree again,
grazing on green pastures,
ready to face the next challenge.

Putrefaction

I could cry
at all I've lost.
The seemingly permanent
putrefaction of my life;
which stinks like
a rotting corpse
too far gone
to revive.
All I can hope
is that the decomposing remains
make good soil,
and I can sprinkle a few seeds
to sprout with a fresh new start
in some distant day.

Useless

I feel utterly useless
like a drunken man
driving a car.
And like him
I should be locked up.
Where they can
feed me,
bathe me,
clothe me,
protect me;
because I am dangerous
and unfit to
function in this world.
My abilities being
as useful as an
incompetent doctor,
or a flat tire.
Still I'm trying to remedy
this situation,
despite my doubts,
of my eventual success.

Gratitude

Did I forget to thank you
for your behavior last night?
Your praise,
compliments,
and the wonderful way you danced with me
gave my self esteem a much needed boost.
Like the first rays of sunlight
returning after an eclipse
my confidence soared
and I felt like a worthwhile human being again.
One who has the resources
to attract a member of the opposite sex
that he can truly love
and banish the dark memories
of lonely nights
of self reproach
to a remote island
where they're never heard from again.

Guilt

I was assaulted by self reproach
for perceived inadequacies and misdeeds.
And my heart sank low
weighed by the gravity
of my supposed failings,
squeezed tight by the
presumed consternation of my peers.

But when I tried to see things realistically
I gingerly concluded that
I had exaggerated the case considerably
and my qualities and deeds
did not warrant reproach at all.
It was just the illusion spun
by my foul mood
like a fog obliterating
the natural contours of the
countryside.

Oh, cursed melancholy
how you spin a web of deceit
and I shall fight you with my intellect
until my last breath does cease.

Deathbed

I feel like I'm on my deathbed,
but I'm physically well.
Instead I suffer from
an emotional sickness
that weighs me down
like cement shoes
and I fear I'm about to hit bottom
all life and enjoyment being
squeezed out of me
like my head was in a vise.
And I know for death to come
it must come by my own hand
but for now I'll just cling
to the hope that treatment brings,
desperate for the scraps of happiness
that my friends and family can provide
like a homeless person collecting coins.
And I hope that I don't feel
driven to end it all,
mostly for my family,
who remind me that
my mood does subside
and I don't have to stay
burning in my bed
forever.

Suicide

You try not to think it,
even though your limbs are made of lead
and your heart is a red, hot coal
searing through your chest.
While your thoughts turn dark
about your ineptitude, your doom
and of your goddamn loneliness
which leaves you cut off from the world
while they cheerfully go about their business.
And you suffer. Just sit and suffer.
Until the thoughts of oblivion creep in
for when the pain of living
exceeds the fear of dying,
and sentimental attachments fade away
suicide becomes a viable option.

Fire

I just can't stand it.
Not the worrisome thoughts,
that seize you as if
you're about to die.
Nor the pessimism,
that punishes you for
who you'd like to be.
Or even the listlessness,
that implodes your dearest dreams.
No, what I really can't stand
is the fire—

a pain that consumes you
like you were burning
from the inside out,
and the searing
flames flickered out
through your pores;
a burning that scorches you
where you once felt pleasure,
so you recoil from
your favorite things;
a burning that leaves your heart
heavy, sorrowful,

and incapable of joy,
like it has been
reduced to nothing
but a pile of hot
ash.

Scatological Poison

Depression gives a fecal heart,
whose stench you just can't stand.
Staining the blood
with scatological poison
until every vessel
in the entire body
burns with the smell
of rotting flesh,
entrapping the soul
in a cadaver
unfit for life;
too cursed for death,
with tears cried in vain,
to the gods of merriment.

III
The Broken Chain

Lost Love

Your splendor lives on in my mind tonight,
The soft glow of your face as you climbed the stairs.
No harsh lines leaped forth in the dim moonlight
Or ungraceful moves, just the curls in your hair.
We laughed and we danced and you held my hand tight,
With a bond that I thought should never end,
Soon the music ended and something so right
Was left hanging in thin air, a prayer to send.
So how was I to know you were attached,
With husband and child that both hold you dear,
All I knew is that we were perfectly matched,
My heart leapt though they say I can't draw you near.
I didn't know what to say or how far I'd get,
But your face drew first blood from the moment we met.

Tissue

I waited patiently for your call
and was met with stone silence.
Here I thought you cared
and we would sail the high seas together.

But now I'm met with your indifference,
and realize that unlike
the other parts of my body
my heart is a most
untrustworthy organ.

Kernel

Your memory haunts me nightly.
Your form silhouetted by the moonlight.

We laughed and talked for hours
of music, futures and Paris.

Until fate tore us apart
and like a shooting star our time was too brief.

And now I'm left with a heart that convulses
at the mere mention of your name.

And like a seedling sleeping under a winter's frost
my love lies dormant, waiting for another day.

Half Moon

Why can I not stand alone,
instead of perennially
needing another?
To hold me,
validate me,
and to love me.

Is it the bombardment
of songs, TV shows, and movies
telling me this is what I need?
Or was I created half made,
like day without the night,
needing someone else
to make me whole.

Whatever it is
it certainly makes
this solitude more difficult.
My thoughts soon turn
to relationships,
like a smoker
to his nicotine,
over and over again,

despite my isolated
situation.

It leaves me unable
to stand strong and independent
like a mighty oak
but rather leaves me
to fade like a weathered orchid
from my long, lonely nights.

Weary

I'm so sad
and weary.
Life has become
like a TV rerun
I've seen it all before
and it just doesn't amuse me.
I'd like to get in my car
and race down the open road,
seeing my blues receding
in the rearview
mirror.

Then I remember your face,
my spirit lifts,
and it all seems worthwhile.
However, like a writing
on the shore
my happiness
doesn't last that long.

So I try to remember that
all things happen
in good time
and that I might

experience good fortune
again.

Maybe I'll see you again
or maybe someone will
take your place.

So if I just push myself
through these dark days
I'll love again,
and laugh again,
enjoying a relationship
to warm my weary
heart.

Discarded Lyre

What good is a heart
with nobody to hold.
Like a fiddler
without his well
worn instrument.

I failed at finding love
since you abandoned me.
And the thought of you
leaves me wanting,
like a song without
it's singer.

So what good is a man
without a woman?
Can he be happy?
Or must he weep each night,
his heart like a dying vow,
at the incompleteness
of his soul.

Everything

It doesn't matter where I go,
what I do,
who I see,
I inevitably end up alone
thinking of you.

Like an abandoned child
crying for his mother
everything seems strange,
every face hostile,
in every place I go.

Like in this barren pub.
So I order another beer,
pray for deliverance,
and the comfort of affection
to brighten my desolate days.

Powerless Passion

I thought I had a love
that would move mountains
and endure throughout the years
but since you left me
I realize it couldn't move a pebble
or outlast a sports season.
Without you I'm left to wonder
what there is to believe in
my friends, family, and faith
seem so pale and unrewarding.

So I'll scribble a few lines
to say how the seasons change
and the harvest we foresee in springtime
can in autumn turn to barren dust.

Fun

I was told to find some enjoyment
like a cat playing with a ball of yarn,
or a dog chasing a stick,
or a lion catching its prey,
or an eagle soaring on high winds.

But I found this difficult
as my heart was shackled and locked
from years of failure
and too few rewards.

Yet I know you hold the key
to unlock my joy
and could end this drought
and lead me with your spirit
to find the place of my
fulfillment.

Eros

He's an unruly youth
shooting his arrows
into unsuspecting victims.
Igniting their loins,
or if he feels more mischievous,
igniting their hearts.
Some say all behavior derives from him
but I find this simplistic and excessive.
Rather he is a key component of human behavior,
driving us on in youth
but becoming less important with age.
A subset of feeling,
like a key log on the emotional fire.

Oh, I pray that the next time he hits me
he also hits the object of my desire as much
and spares me the agony of unrequited love
that aches like my heart was ripped wide open
and only my detached beloved
could heal the gapping wound.

Frost

Its been chilly around here lately
the dead of winter taking hold.
As I stumbled home one snowy night
I caught a glimpse
of a couple kissing
and I remembered
the precious moments we shared
before you were swept away
like the snow from a porch step.
I realize that you may be gone forever
and I'm left here not knowing how you felt.

So as the winds melt the frost
I fear that you are lost.

I would gladly give up the rest of my days
to have just one in which you would stay.

Lottery

I still think of you
every day,
sometimes for most of the day.
And I think I must be crazy
since its been years
since we last saw each other.
But the problem is
that no one has come to take your place,
and I'm beginning to wonder
if anyone can.
Not since you branded
your name on my heart
with a kiss,
a caress,
and the miracle of your personality.

I think the odds of you
coming back
are like me winning the lottery.
But then I remember
that people do buy lottery tickets
and sometimes someone wins.
So I'll sit and hope
I have the winning ticket

beating beneath my breast
with your branded name
being the winning number.

No One But You

I've been looking all around
for a girl just like you.
The problem is
that like fitting a square peg
into a round hole
none of them will do.
Like using the wrong key
to unlock a door
I just can't open your heart.
Try as I might I fail
again and again.
But like a song I just can't
get out of my head
your memory won't fade.
So I'll keep fumbling
through my keys
trying each one on your heart.
Which I know contains a bounty
that is as priceless and plentiful
as the cherry blossoms in spring.

Lost Beneath the Snowfall

How can I see you again
when I don't know where you are.
Like a silver dollar
hidden beneath a snowfall
I come and go and wander
these city streets
never knowing where you lay hidden.
Is it close,
or far?
I do not know.
I just pray for spring
and the melting snow.
So one day the sun may shine down
and glisten on that dollar,
and I may pick it up
put it in my pocket
and hear the phone ring
with the sound of your sweet hello.

A Bottle of Wine

Can I open a bottle
for the two of us.
Pour two glasses,
I'll keep mine here
and put yours in the refrigerator.
Where it can chill
for some later day
when you might return.
Perhaps it will be of better vintage
having aged some time.
We'll laugh and drink
telling of our adventures
as the moonlight shines down
upon your gorgeous smile.
And I start to believe
that love does conquer all
with our having been separated
as if on opposite sides of a wall.

Station

I keep going to the station
watching every train come in,
watch the people get off,
and you're never there;
are you coming?
do you have your ticket?
I miss you so much
its tearing me up inside.
My stomach moans like a lost puppy
and my heart aches like a fractured limb.
So just in case
you might be headed my way
I'll put on my coat,
walk up the hill,
go to the station,
watch one train at a time,
and pray I one day
see your face again.

Caged

I have feelings for you
things I've never felt before.
But like a caged dove
they have no way
of expressing themselves.
So they just flutter away
in a confined space
dreaming of the open sky.
Since you went away
because your commitments went bad,
spoiling like sour milk,
I'm left with a shackled heart
never knowing if it will
sing again.

Or if I'll see your face again
the beauty of which
will surely set that dove free
and leave me happy
as a bird in flight.

Incarnation

Are you an angel in disguise?
Your radiance thus transfigured
as though you were mere flesh and blood.
Your divinity only revealed
through your beautiful smile and eyes,
and the grace in which you
occupy a mortal form,
and move to the rhythms
of wild, Dionysian beats.
Leaving me to yearn for one blissful kiss
and to touch the source
of ecstatic immortality.

Futile

I just can't do anything.
I can't call you, see you,
talk to you, touch you,
kiss you, or caress you.
All I can do is just sit here
and drink beer and smoke cigarettes
pining for your presence.
And praying that what I did
in the past was good enough
for you to return
like the sun returns
after the dark, cold night.

Stone

I always reach for that
which is beyond my grasp
like a drowning man
flailing after a lifesaver.

Your touch,
my mental health,
artistic success,
all prove as elusive as ever.

Until I finally stop flailing
and sink like a stone
drowning in a sea of obscurity.

A Solemn Moment

I saw her gaze at me
with a loving look in her eyes
and I returned in kind.
Our eyes locked
in what seemed an eternal gaze
until she broke away
to speak to her husband

But my heart was ignited
and I knew my days
of peace and contentment
were now over.

Tidal Waters

I lost her somehow.
She was once within my grasp
though someone else
also gripped her tight.
When I conceded to their vows
I left and suffered
howling like a mad dog
at the moon and other couples.
Then one day she was set free
and I thought I could finally
hold her as my own.
But she fled to where
I do not know.

Lost,
like the tidal waters
miss the shore
and I can only hope
they eventually return one day.

Water

I can't live without you
even though I fear I must.
Like a fish pulled out of the water
and lying on the beach
I fear my time is nearly over.
And like that fish needs water
I, my dear, need you.
So as I take my last gasps
I'll check my messages and mail
for some word on where you are.
And maybe they will give me hope
of receiving your life giving presence
and sparing my life
from the death
of the broken hearted.

Frustration

My love for her
almost killed me.
And I'm not sure I won't
meet my end yet.
Hungry, yearning,
searching for the key
to understand the power
her slight frame
has over me.

Death seems quite attractive
as I have concluded
I need her
as an eagle needs the skies.

And if that bird can't fly
it will wither away
thinking dark, catastrophic thoughts.
Until one day it realizes
it will never soar again
and breathes it's last breath.

So I too shall perish
if I never see,
like a child his mother,
those eyes again.

Amour

What good is a life
without love?
Oh, I know
you can get up,
eat, go to work,
keep informed of the
latest news.
But at the end of the day
you still face a
big, lonely bed.
And the memories
of women
who have moved you
but somehow eluded
your grasp.

So you wonder
what do I have to die for
if not a wife and a family.
What is the use of going on
if not for the benefit
of a cherished other.
So like a domestic servant
I will go through the motions
although without love
my heart is not in it.

Silhouette

I can't see your face anymore.
Your form has been reduced to a silhouette,
faded and yellow like an old newspaper.
Your eyes are obliterated,
as is your exquisite smile.
All I'm left with is your words,
but even they are just a faint whisper.
And I strain to hear
a few of the kind things you said
about me and us.
I cling to them for support
to help me through these solitary times,
hoping that you will one day
come close again,
stepping into the sunshine
and driving all shadows away.

Lament of a Loser

I tried my best to make things work.
Chose my words and actions carefully.
Lost myself in the feelings,
got swept up by the passion.
And I thought I did good enough,
that my efforts would bring results.
Though not the best
I stood there honestly
and sincerely
offering the best I could muster.

Then you disappeared.
Across the city, continent, world
I do not know.
And the steady rain
sounds out a lament
for one who is sad,
so very, very sad.

Casket

Its time to lower the flags to half mast.
Bring out the floral wreaths.
Dress all in black.
For there is a solemn procession
leading to the cemetery.
Where a casket will be lowered
and after a few words of remembrance
the dirt will be thrown on top.

For tonight I bury my love for you.
Which was murdered by years of neglect
and still leaves a bitter sweet taste.
But it must be buried
for me to go on
able to embrace another.
And remove any ties
letting me sing finally
of another's charms.

Feelings

The problem is not
with the external circumstances
of the life,
but rather that I have
feelings—
that warm you up
and let you love,
but then spill your blood
with razor sharp
yearnings
and quivering sensitivity.
Consuming you in a fire,
like the grieving widow,
or the bullied youngster.
So if not for this violent
reaction to the events
of my life
I suspect I would
find things not too bad
at all.

But I yearn for that
I could have had,
I should have had.

And for all the lovers
who fate betrayed,
and fight the loneliness
of those whose time
has come and gone.

Top Down

If you love me
you sure have
a funny way
of showing it.
Leaving me on
the side of the highway,
me with my thumb out,
you with the top down,
racing past me
stirring up dust
on my clothes.
And leaving me
to wonder
if you'll eventually
slow down,
turn around,
come back,
and pick me up.
Or will you
race on
leaving me for dead
out here in the desert
my thoughts centered
on you

and my heart burning
as hot as the
scorching sun.

Open Wound

I thought I had defeated it
but like the dead of winter
the frost returned again
chilling my soul,
poisoning my thoughts,
staining my mood
with dark grey colors.

Even though things are going well,
and I don't feel particularly lonely,
all I really need is you.

Yet, that somehow means everything now
so that my possessions and work
don't seem good enough.
And as my spirits sink
the thought of you festers
like an open wound,
one that was nearly healed
but now is ripped wide open.

So I must now try to heal it
with thoughts and pills,
the only things that seem to work,

until it closes up again
and only scar tissue remains.
Even though hearing from you,
something I dare not hope for,
would surely bring
a timely healing
of that open wound.

Off Target

I once loved you deeply
and thought you were
the fairest maiden of all.
Your eyes, smile and
wonderful breasts
were all I thought
beyond compare.
As were your binding heart
and untamable nature.
Most of all I really
thought you loved me too.
Despite the fact you
were already married.

Its funny how the heart
amplifies qualities like
a zoom lens when we're
in love. But like a rabbit
going for a carrot only
to find he's been trapped,
my love for you caught
me in the labyrinth of
unrequited love. Its
an agonizingly lonely

place, full of pining
and despair, and I just hope
my poor heart has
learned it's lesson and
will make better
choices next
time.

Lying in Ash

I guess its finally over,
the fire almost extinguished,
the last dying embers
sputtering out.
And thus our love
lies in ash.
And like after a dying gust of wind
my sail is luffing,
my compass spinning,
as I realize you're
never coming back.
And that you probably
were not even the person
I thought you were.
Yet I feel strangely free
now that the dead weight
of your memory
has been removed
from my neck.
So I can now focus
on what's important.
And like a laboratory rat
who has just learnt
to avoid an electric shock

I can now just leave
you and your memory
alone.

The End of Love

It was a slow, agonizing death.
Full of last gasps and remissions,
love sick poems and midnight obsessions,
but now that it is finally over,
I feel sad, but quite relieved.

Where I expected a wasteland
I now see a lush garden,
full of noncommittal surprises
and blooming flowers just waiting
for my care. As long as they

don't expect too much. For
this projecting of unfulfilled wishes
(youth or love or ecstasy)
on to the opposite sex is
a painful situation indeed.
Better to leave that for
the young and inexperienced.
For maturity demands freedom,
of both mind and heart. So I
gladly leave attachment in my wake.

Romantic Love

It's a funny thing about love.
We crave it.
We enshrine it.
We sing and sing and sing
about it.
But is it really that good for us?
It makes us loose our heads.
Say things we don't mean.
Idealize the mundane.
See things that are not there.
It can ruin careers.
Break up families.
Even cost us our lives.
In short it is an addiction.
Emotional substance abuse.
And in the end what for?
Stable, mutual compatibility
is the best possible outcome.
Why all this melodramatic posturing?
Sure it can make heroes
and heroines out of
normal people.
But is it all worth it?
Could the desired outcome

not be better served by
thoughtful, considered friendship
without all the fireworks?
It's a lot less romantic I know
but as long as there's sexual
tension the chances of success
would be better.
Because that love,
its for suckers.

Childhood Desire

Love is a terrible toddler,
whose parents know no peace.
Unruly, wild, demanding;
expecting immediate gratification
of his desire for his new toy,
the object of his lust,
to make his world seem complete.

Like him love knows no limit
to what it will do for it's object.
Destroying families, careers, lives,
distorting qualities like a salesman,
before it fades like a pair of jeans
that is tossed out in lieu of another.

Leaving one only to hope
that a high degree of affection
exists for the real, accurate person
that once took our breath away
and so a real bond may be forged
as a grown up who loves
and find this adult love
of a much sturdier constitution
then the toddler of our youth.

Stubborn Love

I've tried to forget you,
pretend I have no feelings,
tried to act carefree and unattached,
cursing the day we met
and your sweet, feminine nature.
But like a weed in a garden
I haven't been able to tear out the roots
and like a virus you have
infected my heart
and try as I might
I can't eradicate you
no matter how much echinasia I take.
For you are a stubborn stain
on my feelings
coloring them in love
which secondarily induces
deep suffering
since you are not around
and I'll probably never see you again.
I just hope I can remain rational
about all this emotion,
think through what it means,
and hopefully rub out this stain
so I can just forget about you.

Insomnia

I was up all night,
roaming from room to room.
Looking for something
to amuse myself
in between episodes in bed
where I tossed and turned
like my mattress was made of wood
and my pillow didn't comfort
but rather excited me.

And I worried.
About little things mostly
except for the fact
that I fretted about you.

Outside my window
the moon shone full,
and I wondered if you
could see it too,
and if you realized
how desperately I want
to share it with you
and so many other things
like the inside of my apartment

and the warmness of my bed.
So I hope you call sometime
so I can fall gently
into a slumber of contentment,
knowing you are near.

Fickle

How fickle as a schoolgirl is my heart.
Where once I adored with heart and soul
and gave scarcely a thought to another,
now it all seems stale and old
and I don't know why I even bothered.
Why? Oh, why does my heart always choose
a woman who does not return my affection
leaving me to fend on my own when I most desire
to hold her close and feel her charms.
When will my weary heart strike again,
will it be at some unattainable beauty far above
or at some married lady that tears us apart.
Could I not ask for some simple emotions
reciprocated, in kind, and executed easily,
which leaves all heartache behind
and are blessed with longevity.

Bond

We're connected somehow.
At least that's how
it seems to me.
Long ago we met
and through our eyes
and gestures and laughter
our hearts were bound together
like a performer to his crowd.
And now though we're separated
for a time too long to bear,
I feel our bond will withstand
this test of both time and space
until one day we'll meet again
and will know our hearts survived
this test of strength.

Hate

I hate everything about you, like your
      exquisite smile and tender eyes.
I hate how you look, with your gorgeous
      frame and sweet lips.
I hate your personality, with its accepting
      non judgmental attitude and caring nature.
I hate how you make me feel, full of loving
      songs played in a summer meadow.
I hate the moon and stars, with their romantic
      suggestion and grace and beauty.

But most of all I hate love
      that makes you feel complete
      and whole
      and validated
      and appreciated.

I hate these things because
      I can't have you.
And its a pain
      that cuts me so deeply.

Wrong Side of Love

The cards were stacked from the beginning,
but the dealer cooly dealt our two hands anyways.
I thought I had her, and could taste it,
she acted like she knew I did.
But when we laid our cards down
she had me beat by quite a margin,
so she took my heart and had her way with it,
leaving me to sit solitary with a bottle of bourbon.
Why is it when push comes to shove
I always end up on the wrong side of love?

Secret

We took a stroll
out amongst the sagebrush
while the sun was setting
and the horizon was awash
with crimson flames
and the crescent moon
hung over head
like a chaperone.

We talked for hours
until finally I held your hand
and my heart started thumping
like a bucking stallion
as I realized
you were a perfect match
for my temperament
and interests.

"Stay with me, my love",
I whispered in your ear.
"Forever", you said
as you kissed my forehead.

Soon we were back

amongst the people
that populate our
city, talking and mingling,
going about our business;
and though we're sometimes
torn apart, our
hearts are joined
in an eternal bond,
that is our joy,
that is our secret.

Lovesick

I've got the blues
and they're all about you.
I thought I had put you to rest,
decided I could live without you.
Then someone mentioned your name
and before I knew it
thoughts of you saturated my mind
like a swarm of locusts,
and I needed you
like a sunflower needs the sun.
And I was lying on my bed
my heart burning like a Roman candle
obsessed with your qualities,
beaten up by your memory,
until I thought I would surely perish
if I did not see your smile again.
Sick as consumption,
Love had its way with me.

Smile

My memories of you
drift away
like the sand
by the shore.
Until only a few
remain
but they lead to
one inescapable fact.
And that is I love you dearly
and would love to
make you smile
one more time.

Apparition

I fell in love with you
so deeply,
and so long,
I just hope
the vision of you,
that I cherish,
is not just an apparition.

So that in the unlikely event
you return to me,
and the mist is evaporated
from the window pane,
revealing what lies behind,
I don't find
it is a fiction.

And I learn to love you completely,
like a protege meeting
his beloved mentor,
as the person
I always dreamed
you were.

Sunset Sky

My love for you lingers
like the sunset sky.
You'd think it would have
played itself out,
there being miles
and years between us.
But still it bites me
with a hunger for something
I gave up long ago
after our last goodbye
which at the time I thought
might be a beginning.

And so the women come and go
and I look but don't touch
for the hunger always strikes again.
For when it comes to my heart
all roads lead to you.

River

When our eyes first met
under the milky way
I thought you would be mine,
like a singer has his song.
Then the tides tore us apart
leaving me stranded on a desolate shore,
the seagulls mocking my hemorrhaging heart.
And I'm embarrassed to have loved you,
like a groupie to a star.

A heart denied expression
is like a river that never runs.
Damned up from resistance
it festers in the sun.

About the Author

Paul Kloschinsky was born in Saskatchewan in 1963. He was trained as a physician and practiced as a General Practitioner for a time. For a period in the past he suffered mental health problems. He now lives in Delta, BC. In addition to being a writer, he is also an avid songwriter and photographer. This is his first book.

He has a website at www.kloschinsky.com

ISBN 141209928-5

9 781412 099288